JACQUELINE WO[...]

LOCOMOTION

SCHOLASTIC INC.

New York Toronto London Auckland Sydney
Mexico City New Delhi Hong Kong Buenos Aires

ISBN 0-439-63615-9

12 11 10 9 8 7 6 5 4 3 2 1   4 5 6 7 8 9/0

Printed in the U.S.A.   40

First Scholastic printing, February 2004

Book designed by Gunta Alexander
Text set in Garth Graphic

FOR TOSHI GEORGIANNA AND JUNA FRANKLIN

Name all the people
You're always thinking about
People are poems.
                    —Lonnie C. Motion

LOCOMOTION

Poem Book

This whole book's a poem 'cause every time I try to
tell the whole story my mind goes *Be quiet!*
Only it's not my mind's voice,
it's Miss Edna's over and over and over
Be quiet!

I'm not a really loud kid, I swear. I'm just me and
sometimes I maybe make a little bit of noise.
If I was a grown-up maybe Miss Edna
wouldn't always be telling me to be quiet
but I'm eleven and maybe eleven's just noisy.

Maybe twelve's quieter.

But when Miss Edna's voice comes on, the ideas in my
head go out like a candle and all you see left is this little
string of smoke that disappears real quick
before I even have a chance to find out
what it's trying to say.

So this whole book's a poem because poetry's short and

this whole book's a poem 'cause Ms. Marcus says
write it down before it leaves your brain.
I tell her about the smoke and she says
Good, Lonnie, write that.
Not a whole lot of people be saying *Good, Lonnie* to me

so I write the string-of-smoke thing down real fast.
Ms. Marcus says *We'll worry about line breaks later.*

Write fast, Lonnie, Ms. Marcus says.
And I'm thinking Yeah, I better write fast before Miss
Edna's voice comes on and blows my candle idea out.

ROOF

At night sometimes after Miss Edna goes to bed I go
up on the roof
Sometimes I sit counting the stars
Maybe one is my mama and
another one is my daddy And maybe that's why
sometimes they flicker a bit
I mean *the stars* flicker

LINE BREAK POEM

Ms. Marcus
says
line breaks help
us figure out
what matters
to the poet
Don't jumble your ideas
Ms. Marcus says
Every line
should count.

MEMORY

Once when we was real
little
I was sitting at the window holding my baby sister, Lili
on my lap.
Mama was in the kitchen and Daddy must've
been at work.
Mama kept saying
Honey, don't you drop my baby.

A pigeon came flying over to the ledge
and was looking at us.
Lili put her hand on the glass and the pigeon tried
to peck at it.
Lili snatched her hand away and screamed.
Not a scared scream,
just one of those laughing screams
that babies who can't talk yet like to do.

Mama came running out the kitchen
drying her hands on her jeans.
When she saw us just sitting there, she let out a breath.
Oh, my Lord, she said,
I thought you'd dropped my baby.
I asked
Was I ever your baby, Mama?
and Mama looked at me all warm and smiley.

You still are, she said.
Then she went back in the kitchen.

I felt safe then.
I held Lili tighter.
Maybe if I was eleven then
and if one of my friends had been around,
I would have been embarrassed, I guess.
But I was just a little kid
and nobody else was around.
Just me and Lili and Mama and the pigeons.
And outside the sun
getting bright and warm suddenly
like it'd been listening in.

MAMA

Some days, like today
and yesterday and probably
tomorrow—all my missing gets jumbled up inside of me.

You know honeysuckle talc powder?
Mama used to smell like that. She told me
honeysuckle's really a flower but all I know
is the powder that smells like Mama.
Sometimes when the missing gets real bad
I go to the drugstore and before the guard starts
following me around like I'm gonna steal something
I go to the cosmetics lady and ask her if she has it.
When she says yeah, I say
Can I smell it to see if it's the right one?
Even though the cosmetics ladies roll their eyes at me
they let me smell it.
And for those few seconds, Mama's alive
again.
And I'm remembering
all kinds of good things about her like
the way she laughed at my jokes
even when they were dumb
and the way she sometimes just grabbed me
and hugged me before
I had a chance to get away.

And the way her voice always sounded good
and bad at the same time when she was singing
in the shower.
And her red pocketbook that always had some
tangerine Life Savers inside it for me and Lili

No, I say to the cosmetics lady. *It's not the right one.*
And then I leave fast.
Before somebody asks to check my pockets
which are always empty 'cause I don't steal.

And sometimes I combed Lili's hair
braids mostly but sometimes a ponytail.
Lili would cry sometimes
the kind of crying where no tears came out.
Big faker.
I wouldn't've hurt her head for a million dollars.

Some days
like today and yesterday and probably tomorrow
that's all that's on my mind
Mama and Lili.

Hair and honeysuckle talc powder.

FIRST

First Miss Edna turned the key and
opened her door for me
and said *This ain't much, but it's all I have.*
A living room, a kitchen with a table and three chairs,
a room with just a bed in it and a poster of Dr. J
when he still played for the Sixers and had an Afro.
You'll sleep in here, she said.
Another room down the hall.
No need for you to ever go in there, she said.
I never did.

All along the living room walls there's pictures
of her sons. Grown-up and gone now.

I used to fill up Miss Edna's house with noise.

I used to talk all the time.
I used to laugh real loud and holler especially
when the Knicks won a game 'cause
that don't happen too much.

Be quiet! Miss Edna said.
Hush, Lonnie, Miss Edna said.
Shhhh, Lonnie, Miss Edna said.
Children should be seen but not heard, Miss Edna said.

And my voice got quieter
and quieter
and quiet.

Now some days Miss Edna looks at me and says
You need to smile more, Lonnie.
You need to laugh sometimes
maybe make a little noise.
Where's that boy I used to know,
the one who couldn't be quiet?

Last night this commercial came on TV. It was this white lady making a nice dinner for her husband. She made him some baked chicken with potatoes and gravy and some kind of greens—not collards, but they still looked real good. Everything looked so delicious, I just wanted to reach into that television and snatch a plate for myself. He gave her a kiss and then a voice came on saying *He'll love you for it* and then the commercial went off.

I sat on Miss Edna's scratchy couch wondering if that man and woman really ate that food or just threw it all away.

Now Ms. Marcus wants to know why I wrote that the lady is white and I say because it's true. And Ms. Marcus says *Lonnie, what does race have to do with it,* forgetting that she asked us to use lots of details when we wrote. Forgetting that whole long talk she gave yesterday about the importance of description! I don't say anything back to her, just look down at my arm. It's dark brown and there's a scab by my wrist that I don't pick at if I remember not to. I look at my knuckles. They're real dark too.

Outside it's starting to rain and the way the rain comes down—tap, tapping against the window—gets me to thinking. Ms. Marcus don't understand some things even though she's my favorite teacher in the world. Things like my brown, brown arm. And the white lady and man with all that good food to throw away. How if you turn on your TV, that's what you see—people with lots and lots of stuff not having to sit on scratchy couches in Miss Edna's house. And the true fact is alotta those people are white. Maybe it's that if you're white you can't see all the whiteness around you.

Today's a bad day
Is that haiku? Do I look
like I even care?

GROUP HOME
BEFORE MISS EDNA'S
HOUSE

The monsters that come at night don't
breathe fire, have two heads or long claws.

The monsters that come at night don't
come bloody and half-dead and calling your name.

They come looking like regular boys
going through your drawers and pockets saying

You better not tell Counselor else I'll beat you down.
The monsters that come at night snatch

the covers off your bed, take your
pillow and in the morning

steal your bacon when the cook's back is turned
call themselves The Throwaway Boys, say

You one of us now.
When the relatives stop coming

When you don't know where your sister is anymore
When every sign around you says

Group Home Rules: Don't
do this and don't do that

until it sinks in one rainy Saturday afternoon
while you're sitting at the Group Home window

reading a beat-up Group Home book,
wearing a Group Home hand-me-down shirt

hearing all the Group Home loudness, that
you *are* a Throwaway Boy.

And the news just sits in your stomach
hard and heavy as Group Home food.

HALLOWEEN
POEM

It's Halloween
The first-graders put pumpkin pictures and ghost
drawings all up and down the hallways.
We don't do none of that in fifth grade.
We don't want to.
I mean, we're not supposed to want to.

But sometimes
I do.

There's these two guys I know who sometimes snatch
little kids' trick-or-treat bags. That ain't right.
Once when I was a little kid
this big teenager guy snatched mine.
If I'd a had a big brother,
he would've beat the guy down.

But I
don't.

When people ask how, I say
a fire took them.
And then they look at me like
I'm the most pitiful thing in the world.
So sometimes I just shrug and say
They just died, that's all.

A fire took their bodies.
That's all.

I can still feel their voices and hugs and laughing.
Sometimes.
Sometimes I can hear my daddy
calling my name.
Lonnie sometimes.
And sometimes *Locomotion*
come on over here a minute.
I want to show you something.

And then I see his big hands
holding something out to me.

It used to be the four of us.
At night we went to sleep.
In the morning we woke up and ate breakfast.
Daddy worked for Con Edison.

You ever saw him?
Climbing out of a manhole?
Yellow tape keeping the cars from coming
down the block.
An orange sign that said Men Working.
I still got his hat. It's light blue
with CON EDISON in white letters.

Mama was a receptionist.
When you called the office where she worked,
she answered the phone like this
Graftman Paper Products, how may I help you?
It was her work voice.
And when you said something like
Ma, it's me.
her voice went back to normal. To our mama's voice
Hey Sugar. You behaving? Is the door locked?

That stupid fire couldn't take all of them.
Nothing could do that.

Nothing.

SONNET POEM

Ms. Marcus says mostly sonnets are about love
I think about Mama and Daddy and my sister
how Mama and Daddy are somewhere up above
and Lili's just far away enough for me to miss her.
Ms. Marcus says "sonnet" comes from "sonetto"
and that sonetto means little song or sound
It reminds me of that guy's name—Gepetto
the one who made Pinocchio from wood he found
Ms. Marcus says you gotta write things a lot of times
before they come out sounding the right way
I know this poem's not about love but at least it rhymes
Maybe I'll get the sonnet thing right one day.
If I had one wish I'd be seven years old again
living on President Street, playing with my friends.

HOW I GOT
MY NAME

Whenever that song came on that goes
Come on, baby, do the Locomotion, Mama
would make us dance with her.
We'd do this dance called the Locomotion

when we'd bend our elbows and move
our arms in circles at our sides.
Like our arms were train wheels.
I can see us doing it now—in slow motion.

Mama grinning and singing along
Saying all proud "My kids got rhythm!"
Sometimes Lili got behind me and we'd
do the Locomotion around our little living room. Till

the song ended.
And we fell out on the couch
Laughing. Mama would say
You see why I love that song so much, Lonnie?

See why I had to make it your name?
Lonnie Collins Motion, Mama would say.
Lo Co Motion
Yeah.

DESCRIBE SOMEBODY

Today in class Ms. Marcus said
Take out your poetry notebooks and describe somebody.
Think carefully, Ms. Marcus said.
You're gonna read it to the class.
I wrote, Ms. Marcus is tall and a little bit skinny.
Then I put my pen in my mouth and stared down
at the words.
Then I crossed them out and wrote
Ms. Marcus's hair is long and brown.
Shiny.
When she smiles it makes you feel all good inside.
I stopped writing and looked around the room.
Angel was staring out the window.
Eric and Lamont were having a pen fight.
They don't care about poetry.
Stupid words, Eric says.
Lots and lots of stupid words.
Eric is tall and a little bit mean.
Lamont's just regular.
Angel's kinda chubby. He's got light brown hair.
Sometimes we all hang out,
play a little ball or something. Angel's real good
at science stuff. Once he made a volcano

for science fair and the stuff that came out of it
looked like real lava. Lamont can
draw superheroes real good. Eric—nobody
at school really knows this but
he can sing. Once, Miss Edna took me
to a different church than the one
we usually go to on Sunday.
I was surprised to see Eric up there
with a choir robe on. He gave me a mean look
like I'd better not
say nothing about him and his dark green robe with
gold around the neck.
After the preacher preached
Eric sang a song with nobody else in the choir singing.
Miss Edna started dabbing at her eyes
whispering *Yes, Lord.*
Eric's voice was like something
that didn't seem like it should belong
to Eric.
Seemed like it should be coming out of an angel.

Now I gotta write a whole new poem
'cause Eric would be real mad if I told the class
about his angel voice.

Epistle Poem

Hey Pops,

Today our teacher showed us this poem by this poet guy named Langston Hughes. It made me remember something. That long time ago when you read us that good-night poem about that guy who loved his friend. And it made me kinda think that maybe Langston Hughes is the same guy who wrote that one because his name sounded familiar. Underwater familiar—like I dreamed it sort of. I'm not gonna try to explain. I figure you understand. The only thing about what Ms. Marcus read was it wasn't a *poem* poem. She said it's called an epistle poem and it was a letter. I didn't know a letter could be a kind of poem. So now I'm writing one to you to say that even though we can't do stuff like go to the park on our bikes or eat hot dogs from that cart where the guy who always wore the Yankees cap yelled at me for being a Mets fan but gave us a discount if we bought four hot dogs—and we always did—and ate them standing there arguing with him. Even when the Mets lost again and again. I just wanted to say that even though we can't do that kind of stuff no more, I haven't forgot none of it. I'm gonna go see if I can find that poem about that guy loving his friend. I hope it's by Langston Hughes.

—Love, Locomotion

ROOF
POEM II

Up here the sky goes on and on like something
you could fall right up into.

And keep falling.
Fall so fast
and so far
and for so long you don't
have to worry about where you're gonna live next,

where you gonna be

if somebody all of a sudden
changes their mind about living with you.

Up here, you could
just let your mind take you
to all kinds of beautiful places
you never been before in real life
Tahiti, Puerto Rico, Spain,
Australia with all those kangaroos hopping around
and then you can come on back
and call the place you come back to

home.

ME, ERIC, LAMONT & ANGEL

Once I saw a house fall down on a lady, Lamont says.
That ain't nothing, Angel says. *Once I saw this dog
get hit by a car. He went way up in the air and
when he came down again,*
he got up and ran away. But he stopped at the corner,
Angel says.
And died.

Eric squints up his eyes.
Looks out over the school yard.
The sky's real blue and no wind's blowing.
I shake my head, trying to shake that dog out of it.
Once I saw a little boy, Eric says, all mysterious.
And then in my dream, he was a man.

We all look at him and don't say nothing.
Far away, I hear some girls singing real slow and sad
Her mother, she went upstairs too.
Saying daughter oh daughter
what's troubling you . . .

That ain't no tragedy, Angel says, giving Eric a look.

More than what Lonnie seen, Eric says, grinning at me.

In my head I see a fire. I see black windows.
I hear people hollering. I smell smoke.
I hear a man's voice saying *I'm so sorry.*
I hear myself screaming.

Never seen nothing, I say.

FAILING

I got a 39 on my math test
'cause
I don't understand numbers
'cause
you say 1 + 1 = 2 and I go why? You say just
'cause
like just 'cause somebody said it means it's the truth.
And since I don't believe the things people say is
always the truth
'cause
sometimes people lie
it's hard to understand math.

New boy comes in our classroom today
Ms. Marcus says
Say good morning, Clyde, and the new boy says
Good mornin', y'all
and the whole class falls out laughing
so hard, Ms. Marcus taps her pointer on the desk,
her face so mad it's purple
R-e-s-p-e-c-t, she says
Respect! we repeat the way
she taught us to—a thousand times ago.

New boy's looking down at the floor
looks real sad, says *I'm sorry, ma'am*
and the class tries hard not to laugh
but some laugh spills out of us anyway.
You've nothing to be sorry about, Ms. Marcus says.

Lamont whispers *He should be sorry he's so country*
Eric says *Look at his country clothes*
New boy knows
they're whispering about him,
puts one foot behind his leg
like he wants to crawl right inside himself.
He's wearing high-water pants, light blue socks,
a white shirt
buttoned all the way up

tight around his neck
Check
Eric says
Check out his country hat
New boy's holding the hat in his hands
Granddaddy hat in his hands the kind
with the black band going around gray felt
New boy looking like he wish he could
just melt right on outa the room.

I wake up with my stomach all bunched, throw up
two times. Miss Edna gives me three Tums,
the spearmint ones
but the stomach pains don't go away and I don't want
    breakfast.
Not cereal. Not oatmeal. Not even pancakes.
Miss Edna frowns, presses her hand to my forehead,
fixes
me a bed on the couch.
It's December ninth, she says.
I don't look at her, just go back into the bathroom
Nothing but bitter stuff comes up. And tears.

I hear Miss Edna calling her job saying she won't
be coming in. I hear her say *Dear Lord, remember me.*
I hear her putting water on to boil
and smell the ginger she's chopping up to make me
    some tea.

It's been four years, Miss Edna says to the Lord
How long will he carry this burden?

I see my old house on President Street
the window frames black from fire. Glass everywhere.
I hear people screaming and crying.
I see the firemen wearing oxygen masks and shaking
    their heads.

It's cold out. There's water everywhere.
And two of Lili's dolls—burnt and wet on the ground.
I hear Lili screaming for Mama
or maybe it's me.

There's relatives down south who don't have room
for us. There's church people who take us for a while
     then pass
us on to more church people until there ain't no more
     church people
just group homes where people come sometimes to
     bring us food and
toys and read us books they wrote. Then go on home
     to their own families.
There used to be four of us
Mama, Daddy, Lili and me. At night we went to sleep.
In the morning we woke up and ate breakfast.
That was four years ago.

I lean my head over the toilet bowl
and more of the bitter stuff comes.

LIST POEM

Blue kicks—Pumas
Blue-and-white Mets shirt
Mets hat
A watch my daddy gave me
Black pants but not dressy—they got side pockets
Ten cornrows with zigzag parts like Sprewell's
A gold chain with a cross on it from Mama—under
my shirt
White socks *clean*
One white undershirt *clean*
White underwear *clean*
A dollar seventy-five left pocket
Two black pens
A little notebook right pocket
All my teeth inside my mouth
One little bit crooked front one
Brown eyes
A little mole by my lip
Lotion on so I don't look ashy
Three keys to Miss Edna's house back pocket
Some words I wanted to remember
written on my right hand
Leftie
Lonnie

LATE SATURDAY AFTERNOON IN HALSEY STREET PARK

Shoot hoops with me, Dog
Eric says. Throws me the ball.
Where you been all day?

Pigeon

People all the time talking about how much they hate pigeons 'cause pigeons fly by and crap on their heads and then somebody always says *That's good luck! That's good luck!* so you don't feel all stupid going through your pockets tryna find a tissue to wipe it off and you never find one 'cause you don't be carrying tissues like an old lady so you gotta walk up to some old lady with that pigeon crap on your head and ask her for a tissue and she just goes *Don't worry, that's good luck* like everybody else and it makes you hate those sky roaches 'cause they're everywhere in the city so you better duck if they fly over your head or else

But

This guy Todd that lives next door to Miss Edna's building got a pigeon coop on his roof and sometimes I go up there and watch Todd waving this huge white sheet till all the pigeons come swooping and flying above us— back and forth and up and down making those croaky pigeon sounds. Those days I'm not scared about pigeon crap on my head because the way they fly—just slow back and forth and the sun getting all bright orange behind them and them making those sounds that after a while sound a little bit like a song—all of it together makes you look up into the sky and believe in everything you ever wanted to believe in. Especially with Todd standing there waving that white sheet and his brown face all broken out in the biggest smile you ever seen on a teenager.

SOMETIMES POEM

Miss Edna gets her paycheck the second Friday
of every month and we go to C-Town. Sometimes
the Twinkies go on sale three for five dollars and
    Miss Edna says
Get three. You know how we love ourselves some
    Twinkies, Lonnie
And her smile gets big and so does mine.
We go up to the cash register with all our food.
When I put the Twinkies on the counter, the checkout
    lady says
I guess your son likes Twinkies, huh?
And Miss Edna looks at me sideways.
Then she smiles and says
Yeah, I guess he does.

Miss Edna got two other sons—Rodney and Jenkins.
Jenkins's off fighting in the war.
Rodney, he lives upstate and once a month
Miss Edna goes up there and visits him. She packs up
fried chicken and potato salad and
makes a pound cake. Puts it all
in a shopping bag and the shopping bag smells
like lots of good things.
She leaves two chicken legs and some potato
salad on a plate for me when
I don't
go with her but sometimes
I do
and we take a bus all the way up where there's
mountains and grass everywhere.
Lots of trees too.

Miss Edna can't visit her other son, so she prays.
I find her like that sometimes—on her knees in her
    room with her hands
pressed together, her eyes closed.
Dear Lord, I heard her say once
Keep Jenkins safe and don't let too many people die in this
    war.

The war's on the other side of the world.

But Jenkins is fighting in it.
And Miss Edna's praying about it.
So I guess it's the same as if it was right here
in our city
in our house
in Miss Edna's room
Everywhere.

Ever been south? We
used to go all the time. That's
another poem.

Cloudy out and just a little bit of rain spraying
across our faces, some kids got their coats
hanging from their heads. Some shivering but we all
in the school yard 'cause the lunchtime teacher
   stuck her hand
out the door, frowned and said *Okay, go on out, I guess*

New boy's across the yard talking
to a little girl look like him, she
got high-water pants on too
only hers are pink and she got brown shoes that look
about a hundred years old. Her hair in four
big braids like Lili likes to wear sometimes maybe
she's Lili's same age. New boy puts his arm
around her shoulders and they just stand there like
that looking out over the yard. Watching
them I feel something in the back of my throat
close up and choke at me. Then slide on
down to my stomach and make itself some tears.

No rain but the sky
is this strange color—silver almost and the sun
white—like this white ball behind a piece
of silver foil. You could look
right at the sun and not go blind.
It's watery like that.
Safe to look at today.

That's what I'm thinking when Eric
comes up to where I'm sitting
in the school yard 'cause it's lunchtime
The kind of day
when I don't want
to do nothing
but go somewhere and write
Writing makes me remember.
It's like my whole family comes back again
when I write. All of them right
here like somebody pushed the Rewind button
And that's what I'm writing when Eric
comes up to where I am—in the far back
of the school yard
Writing and eating my grilled cheese sandwich I snuck
from the cafeteria. *What you doing?* Eric
wants to know. He's wearing a leather jacket

like the kind I want to get one day—brown
with black sleeves
His own name across the whole front
E-R on one side
of the zipper
I-C on the other.
I close up my notebook. Say *Nothing*.
When I don't want to be scared of Eric I think
about how he sings. Bird Eric. Angel Eric. Churchboy.
Don't look like Nothing to me, Eric says.
His voice is hard. His eyes get real mean.
He calls me a punk and some other words I don't
want to even write down.
I don't know why he's so evil some days
with his stupid angel voice
and mean-as-the-devil ways.

They tell me and Lili we can sit in a room and talk—
    catch up, the tall lady says and I ask
for how long and the tall lady says *An hour* then Lili's
    new mama says
An hour. That's plenty of time.

I guess Lili's new mama and the tall lady never had a
    brother they didn't live with no
more 'cause if they did they'd know an hour goes by
    like three minutes or maybe even
faster than that.

Sometimes I go to Lili's new mama's house to visit.
I take the #52 bus and then I transfer for the #69 bus
    and then
I get off and walk five blocks.

But sometimes Lili's new mama don't want me to
    come there
and she don't want to bring Lili to Miss Edna's house
so we meet at the agency. Like today.

The agency's a gray building. It's ugly
It smells like Ajax. The floors got scuffs on them but
they shine. There's only a couple windows though
and not a whole lot of light coming in.

I look at Lili a long time and for a long time
she looks right back at me. She's
wearing a pink dress with flowers on it. She's got pink
    ribbons in her hair,
real pretty. My sister's real pretty. She's got little
dimples on her cheeks and her eyes
are big and round even when she's not surprised.
They're light brown too
like Mama's.

Mama.
Some days I don't think about her
and some days I do. Daddy too.
Not the fire though.
I shake my head when those thoughts come
Shake them out real fast.

I pull on the sleeves of my suit jacket. It's brown
and getting too small but Miss Edna says you gotta
look presentable for Saturday visits so Miss Edna gave
    me twenty dollars
for the girl across the street to braid my hair.

Before I left the group home, this boy named Andre
    pierced my ear for me.
Miss Edna lets me wear the earring but on Saturdays I
    take it out so

Lili's new mama won't look at me with that look that
    says
You look like a bad boy to me.

Lili's new mama didn't want no boys
Just a sweet little girl. Nobody told me that
I just know it.
Not a lot of people want boys
Not foster boys
that ain't babies.
Miss Edna took me 'cause
she already raised two sons. Said she knew what to do
if I didn't act right. Said she knew more about boys
    than she did
about girls. The first day I heard
her ask the tall lady
He ever been arrested?
And the tall lady said
Uh-uh. Not Lonnie. He's quiet. Good.
Quiet is good
It's hard to be quiet all the time though.
And sometimes Miss Edna gets to yelling at me.
And that yelling ain't quiet either.

You found God yet, Lonnie? Lili says.
She's got on little white gloves.
One of her hands is holding a Bible.

I wasn't looking for Him, I say back.
Then I smile so that Lili knows I'm just goofing.
But she don't
smile back at me. Instead, she looks real serious.
God is everywhere, she says. *He comes in your heart if
    you let Him.*
She sounds real grown-up. Like she's twenty-five
instead of eight.
But then her eyes get all watery.
You find God, Lonnie, she says, *then maybe me and you
    can be together again.*

Maybe a real big brother would tell her it'd take a lot
    more than that.
Tell her that her new mama's never gonna take me in
and some days I can't imagine living anyplace else but
in Miss Edna's house.
Some days I look around my room and say,
*Locomotion, stop thinking about moving on 'cause
this is home.*

But

My eyes just get all watery too and I wipe them
real fast. Then I turn toward the one
little window in our room so that Lili won't
see more tears already starting to come down.

Yeah, Lili, I say. *I'm gonna go looking for Him, okay?*

Then Lili gives me her Bible and kisses me on the
   cheek.
She has a big smile on her face. *You're the best brother,*
   she says
the best brother in the whole world. In the whole galaxy.

I look down at the Bible and let myself start grinning.

That Lili's something else.

JUST NOTHING
POEM

Sometimes Ms. Marcus makes me sick!
Now everybody's head's bent over their notebooks.
This girl LaTenya that I like a little bit
got her tongue sticking outa
the side of her mouth like she's really concentrating.
Like she knows just what to write.

Even Lamont and Eric writing all serious like
they know exactly what they're doing.
Me? I'm slouching
waiting for that stupid teacher to say
"Sit up straight, Lonnie."
Me? I'm slouching down and staring
out at the rain, city
so gray you'd think we live inside a big old gray box.
Clouds hanging so low they look
like aluminum foil
Reynolds Wrap sky.
Me? I'm waiting for her to say
"Stop daydreaming, Lonnie."
I want to yell today.
Get real mad at somebody.
I want to punch something. Hard.
Maybe punch somebody.

Me? I want to yell
What family?!

It's thundering now. Lightning too.
When the thunder comes hard, everybody jumps.
Then some people laugh.
Me? I don't jump or laugh
like a stupid person. Thunder don't scare me none.
Me? I'm just sitting here with nothing
to say wishing Ms. Marcus would vaporize
like the people do on *Star Trek.*
Lonnie, she says. *Are you writing about your family
or just daydreaming?*
Me? I ain't got nothing to say today.
Just feel like sitting here
Watching the rain come down
and down

> and

> > down.

GOD POEM

There's some glass on Miss Edna's roof
You gotta make sure you don't sit on it in the dark.
It's from people roofing bottles
You finish your soda or whatever and

you throw your bottle on a roof
Sometimes people miss.
Once this bottle came speeding back down and broke
in a million pieces

This boy Isaiah had to go to the hospital
'cause glass went in his eye.
And nosy old Miss Portia who lives across
the street kept saying

See? See? I told y'all somebody was
gonna get hurt one of these days.

Some of this glass is probably mine.
If I get cut on the butt it's my own fault.
But I come up here anyway.

Even when it's cold like tonight.
I just got to zip my jacket way up
and pull my hat way down
then I'm all right.

There's a fat moon and enough stars to read Lili's
    Bible by
I don't understand a lot of the words
and I'm waiting for God to show Himself to me
Not for me so much—for Lili.

Yeah, I guess, for me too.

ALL OF A SUDDEN, THE POEM

Today Angel said he was writing a book
of poems called *All of a Sudden, The Sun*
Ms. Marcus's smile got so big
you could see her back teeth.
Angel got all show-offy then, saying
every poem is gonna be about
how sometimes the sun just comes out when you don't
expect it to—like when
it's raining and stuff. And Ms. Marcus
just kept smiling and shaking her head and saying
Wonderful, brilliant, excellent, good for you, Angel until
other kids caught on to all the smiling she was doing
just for Angel and started talking
about books they were gonna write like
All of a Sudden, The Moon and
All of a Sudden, The School and
All of a Sudden, The Pepsi Cola Can until
the titles got so stupid, Ms. Marcus stopped
smiling, told us poetry was over
for the day. Said it was time
for math.
And I didn't even care because
Angel's idea wasn't the best idea

I ever heard in the world even if
Ms. Marcus thought so.
She don't know everything anyway.
Probably wouldn't know a good poet if . . .
If . . .

If nothing.

Some days I hate poetry.
The way the good ideas be going
to somebody else.

Hey Dog

Hey Dog!
That's how you call your boys.
Hey Dog. You want to hoop?
Then you and your dogs are throwing
the ball around and talking about
girls and ballplayers and stuff
you're gonna have one day
A red car
some slamming kicks
a shearling coat
a pocket full of money
a pretty girl
a satellite dish *and* cable
on and on you and your dogs
two college degrees, straight A straight up
a phat deal with the Lakers
no, the Knicks
no, the Nets
Nah—the Nets ain't nothing.
What you talking about, Dog? The Nets got game.
Yeah, a game of checkers!!
Game of tag, maybe.
Game of pin the tail on the donkey!
Just grinning and talking junk
shooting hoops

not even knowing where
or when people started calling the people
they like to be around *Dog*
but liking it and feeling good when
your dog slaps your hand, gives you a quick hug, says
What's up, Dog?

OCCASIONAL POEM

Ms. Marcus says that an occasional poem is a poem
written about something
important
or special
that's gonna happen
or already did.
Think of a specific occasion, she says—*and write about it.*

Like what?! Lamont asks.
He's all slouched down in his seat.
I don't feel like writing about no occasion.

How about your birthday? Ms. Marcus says.
*What about it? Just a birthday. Comes in June and it ain't
June,* Lamont says. *As a matter of fact,*
he says, *it's January and it's snowing.*
Then his voice gets real low and he says
*And when it's January and all cold like this
feels like June's a long, long ways away.*

The whole class looks at Ms. Marcus.
Some of the kids are nodding.
Outside the sky looks like it's made out of metal
and the cold, cold air is rattling the windowpanes
and coming underneath them too.

I seen Lamont's coat.
It's gray and the sleeves are too short.
It's down but it looks like a lot of the feathers fell out
a long time ago.
Ms. Marcus got a nice coat.
It's down too but real puffy so
maybe when she's inside it
she can't even tell January from June.

Then write about January, Ms. Marcus says, *that's*
an occasion.
But she looks a little bit sad when she says it
Like she's sorry she ever brought the whole
occasional poem thing up.

I was gonna write about Mama's funeral
but Lamont and Ms. Marcus going back and forth
zapped all the ideas from my head.

I guess them arguing
on a Tuesday in January's an occasion
So I guess this is an occasional poem.

HAIKU POEM

Ms. Marcus wants to
see all my poems. No way.
Some things just your own.

It's lunchtime.
I just ate a cheeseburger with french fries and some applesauce
which means today's a good lunch day 'cause
sometimes they put stuff on your tray and you don't know what
it is but you eat it anyway 'cause
Mr. Hungry don't care.

I'm shooting hoops by myself, liking the way the ball sounds
Swish
when it goes through the basket without touching the rim
and I'm by myself too 'cause both Eric and Lamont are absent.
It's Friday.
Maybe they took themselves a three-day weekend.

LaTenya comes over, walking all slow.
She's wearing her hair in lots of braids
and she even got some cowry shells in some of them.
And the cowry shells make a little bit of noise
A nice noise.

You know you got some pretty eyes, LaTenya says to me

My eyes just eyes but LaTenya's looking at them
like she's seeing them for the first time
and maybe later on I'll go back to Miss Edna's house
and look in the mirror at my eyes
try to see what she's seeing.

Thanks, I say. And then I take another shot and miss
and LaTenya laughs
Guess they can't see the basket so good though, huh?
she says.
But she's only joking.
Then she leans against the school yard fence
and I take a few more shots
and they go in
Swish. Swish. Swish.

I want to say *I found God, Lili.*
And throw up my hands.
And grin like somebody's big old fool.

You don't just get to write a poem once
You gotta write it over and over and over
until it feels real good to you
And sometimes it does
and sometimes it doesn't
That's what's really great
and really stupid
about poetry.

ERIC POEM

Lamont comes back on Monday morning
but Eric doesn't
Ms. Marcus stands up in front of the class and coughs.
Not a real cough. The kind of cough
grown-ups get when they'd rather not
be talking to you.
The tall lady from the agency gets that cough
when I ask her if me and Lili ever gonna live
together again.

Ms. Marcus says *I have some sad news*
Eric is in the hospital.
She says he has a disease
and some of his cells are shaped funny.
And sometimes, she says, *that makes his life very painful.*
Can you catch it from him? Angel asks, looking scared.
'Cause me and him was hanging a lot and I don't want
no disease.
No, Ms. Marcus says. *It's not contagious.*
She draws a shape on the board.
Does anybody know what a sickle is, she says.
Nobody raises their hand.
I know what a sickle is. Slaves used it to cut
sugarcane and stuff.
I know a lot of other kids know too

but our minds are busy wrapping themselves around
    Eric
and all the pain in his body and how
we never knew he had no disease.
Ms. Marcus explains what a sickle is.
Then she says, *Eric has sickle-cell anemia.*
She coughs again and says
It's a disease that's common . . .
She stops talking
looks around the room for a minute
then she kind of whispers
among African Americans.

There's six Puerto Ricans in our class—
Manny, Lourdes, Jillian,
Samantha, Carlos, and Sophia.
There's two Dominicans—Angel and Maritza.
Gina and Cara are from Trinidad and
Guy is from Jamaica.
All the rest of us are from right here.
All the rest of us are African American.
Everyone looks around the room at everybody else.

Do you die with that, Lamont wants to know.
Not directly, Ms. Marcus says. But she doesn't explain
and nobody asks any more questions about dying.

How long they gonna keep him

in the hospital? Somebody else wants to know.

I don't know, Ms. Marcus says.
His mother doesn't know yet, Ms. Marcus says.
Let's hope not long though, Ms. Marcus says.
Ms. Marcus says.
Ms. Marcus says.
Ms. Marcus says and the words circle
round the room, bounce off the walls
keep zooming
past my head.
Zip! Zap!
Like they're banging against it.

I thought, Ms. Marcus says
we could make him a card.

I take a deep breath and put my head down on my
    desk.
I try not to think of Eric's angel voice singing in
    church.
I try not to think of us shooting hoops together at
    lunchtime.
My throat feels all choky though anyway.
My whole body feels bent out of shape and strange.
The last time Miss Edna came home and found me
crying she said *Think*
about all the stuff you love, Lonnie.

Let those things fill your head.

Popsicle
Icicle
Bicycle

    Sickle cell.

Popsicle
Icicle
Bicycle

    Sickle cell.

Lamont comes in mad on Wednesday.
Ms. Marcus makes believe she doesn't see him sitting
over there with his arms folded,
his face all scrunched up staring out the window, his
back the only thing facing front.
Let's take out our poetry notebooks, Ms. Marcus says.
I want to work on haiku again today.
I don't like forms. I like free verse when you can write
anything you want
any way you want but Ms. Marcus says
there's a time for form and a time for free verse
which I think is a stupid, very teacher thing to say.
I ain't writing no poetry, Lamont says. *No black guys be
writing poetry anyway.*
I already have my poetry notebook open but I close it
   real fast.
What about Richard Wright, Ms. Marcus says. *And
   Langston Hughes.*
Angel says *I know Richard Wright. He lives on my block.
His mom's name's Mrs. Wright.*
I know Langston Hughes too, Angel says.
I see a little smile on Lamont's face but he's still
sitting turned away
from the whole class.

Both of them died a long time ago, Ms. Marcus says. But she's kinda smiling too.

How's he gonna be dead and still live on my block? Angel wants to know.

He gives Ms. Marcus a look like she's lost her mind.

Pablo died, Angel says. *He got shot by somebody last year. But not Richard.*

Richard Wright was right there playing basketball last Saturday. He could slam-dunk.

But the rim's bent so it don't really count.

*Richard Wright—the poet—*Ms. Marcus says *wrote haiku. Langston Hughes—the poet—wrote all kinds of poetry.*

Richard Wright also wrote novels.

Whole books? I ask. I didn't know poets could write whole stories.

Whole books, Ms. Marcus says.

Lamont doesn't say anything but I see his head turning front a little bit.

He make a lot of money? Angel wants to know.

Ms. Marcus picks up a book off of her desk.

He wrote because he loved writing, she said.

That's what matters.

Not if you broke, Angel says. The whole class laughs.

Even Lamont.

But he looks over where Eric's empty chair is and then

he stops laughing real fast.

Do you think poor people aren't happy? Ms. Marcus says.

Angel shrugs. *I don't know. Don't know any poor people.*

But when you see those pictures on TV of those kids who

they want you to send money to,

they don't look happy to me.

They just look hungry and sad.

Ms. Marcus doesn't say anything. She looks stuck.

Real stuck and I feel

kinda sorry for her.

Let's take out our poetry notebooks, she says again.

Everybody but Lamont takes out their notebooks and

just sort of stares down at them.

Ms. Marcus sits down at her desk.

She lets out a deep breath

pushes her hair away from her face

looks out at all thirty-two of us

shakes her head.

And for a long, long time just stares
down at her hands.

Hip Hop Rules the World, Lamont said
grinning like somebody had told him
he'd just won the lotto.

But all it was was Ms. Marcus saying
Of course rap is poetry!
One of the most creative forms.

So now Lamont's writing lyrics
and bopping his head
and every chance he gets

saying
Hip Hop Rules the World
and

It's one of the most creative forms
and
Hey Dog! Guess who else is a poet now!

Photographs

There's two of me and Lili.
We were little then, dressed up at Easter time
Big smiles—me with two front teeth missing
and my head shaved Easter clean.

Here's Mama and Daddy dancing,
Mama's blurry foot lifted up in the air.
Look how she's laughing.

When I look at the picture I can hear it.

Here's the four of us
Everybody smiling at the camera but
me. I'm looking away from it
frowning
Like I see something coming
that ain't good.

He says *My name is*
Clyde not New Boy, not Country,
not Straw Head Cotton-Picker Dirt-Eater Bumpkin.
Just Clyde. Easy to say. Easy to remember.
Why don't soma y'all try to use it sometime.
After all, he says
I thought city people was supposed to be smart.

HAPPINESS POEM

This afternoon I come home to find
Miss Edna dancing with the broom
The broom's swishing across the floor and Miss Edna
got a tight hold on its blue handle and singing
along with the radio. She's kind
of soft-shoeing the poor broom back and forth
across the kitchen floor like her mind
is gone. That's what I'm thinking, praying
Please Lord don't let Miss Edna's mind be gone
'cause I was just getting used to living here
Please Lord me and her don't always get along but
she's all I got right now when Miss Edna turns
to me with the biggest smile I seen in a long time
and says *My Rodney is coming for Easter*
My Rodney is bringing himself on home for a while
Then she's swish-swishing off again with me
just standing there feeling the relief lift me up and
set me right back down in Miss Edna's kitchen again.

When I was born I didn't even
weigh four pounds, Mama used to tell me.
See this chicken I'm about to cut up and fry?
You were even smaller than it. Doctors said
there's a little bit we can do but mostly you
have to hope hard
and pray.
Mama cut the wing off the chicken, rinsed
it under the faucet, patted it dry—real gentle
like she was deep remembering.
So I hoped and prayed and sat by that tiny
baby every hour of every day for weeks
and more weeks. Doctors said it's his lungs,
they're just not ready for the world yet. Can't
take a breath in. Can't let one out. So I breathed
for you, trying to show you how, I
prayed to those lungs, Mama said. *Grow!*
The chicken was cut up, spiced up, dipped
in flour and ready to fry. Mama touched each piece
still real gentle before she slipped it into the hot
oil. *Then you were four pounds, five pounds, six pounds*
bigger than this chicken. My big little baby boy
not even two months old and already
a survivor.

Lili's New Mama's House

The #52 bus takes a long time coming and even though it's the first day of spring it's still a little cold so when the #69 comes real fast, I think That's God. And when the heat's turned up real high inside the bus and I ain't shivering no more, I think That's God too.

And then I'm walking the blocks to Lili's new mama's house and when I get there, I see Lili standing at the window waving and grinning and I think
There's God.
Lili's new mama lives on a pretty block with trees and brownstone houses that all look alike so if you don't know the address you end up knocking on a stranger's door even if you been there a couple of times before. Now I know Lili's mama's house is the one with yellow curtains on the second floor and, most times, with Lili in the window.

We sit in the living room. It smells like lemon and Lili says, "That's what we clean the floor with." The floors are made of wood and there's pretty rugs in different spots. Not a whole lot of furniture but enough to find a nice place to sit. I don't lean back though cause Lili's new mama will give me a look. There's chocolate chip cookies and two glasses of milk on the coffee table. I take one cookie and eat it real slow even though I

want to take a whole bunch at one time. Then I take
a little sip of milk and make sure to set my glass back
down on the coaster thing 'cause I know Lili's new
mama is watching me from the kitchen. There's bright
sun coming in through the big windows and the house
is like this yellow-gold color and warm. Even though
Lili's new mama doesn't like me, I'm glad that my sister
has such a nice place to sleep at night. And I'm glad
she has a nice room to sit in and eat chocolate chip
cookies and drink milk outa blue glasses that make
you think of nights up on the roof in the summertime.

God's in this room, I whisper to Lili.
She looks at me a minute without saying anything.
Then she smiles.
God is everywhere, I say.

And with the sun coming in the room that way
and my sister smiling so big and the plate
of cookies there if you want them, just take one
at a time and chew it slow
I feel Him, right there beside us.

Church

On Sundays, the preacher gives everyone a chance
to repent their sins. Miss Edna makes me go

to church. She wears a bright hat
I wear my suit. Babies dress in lace.

Girls my age, some pretty, some not so
pretty. Old ladies and men nodding.

Miss Edna every now and then throwing her hand
in the air. Saying *Yes, Lord* and *Preach!*

I sneak a pen from my back pocket,
bend down low like I dropped something.

The chorus marches up behind the preacher
clapping and humming and getting ready to sing.

I write the word HOPE on my hand.

Takes the soccer ball
around the school yard eight times
His feet are magic.

TEACHER OF THE YEAR

The news people from Channel 7 Eyewitness
News came to our school. 'Cause guess what?
Ms. Marcus is the Teacher of the Year.
Ms. Marcus smiling all proud brought them
right into our classroom and we all crowded
around the cameras, pulling at the mikes, making
faces into the camera, getting into trouble.

Me and Angel was standing together and we

heard the newsman talking to Ms. Marcus about
inner-city and underserved and Angel looked at me
That's the nice way of saying poor, he said.
*What poor person's daddy can afford to buy him
hundred-dollar kicks?* He held up his foot to the camera
showing off his new sneaker. The newsman heard
him. He put the mike in Angel's face and said

Tell me about this man.

He don't live with us, Angel said, *but he comes every
     night to
read me and my sister a book or to watch some TV with
     us before
we go to bed.* Angel got quiet after that, pushed the mike
away from his face. For a minute, the newsman

79

just stood there—then quick fast, he turned to me
asked *What do you like about your teacher?* Someone
behind me said math and poetry. I shushed her.

Not math, I said. *Just the poetry.*

Well, why don't you read us something,
the newsman said.
His hair looked like it was sprayed with a whole can
of hairspray. It looked hard and shiny. Everybody
ran to get their poetry books saying *Me, Me,* but the
newsman kept looking at me. *No,*
he said. *I'd like to hear something
from this gentleman.* I looked at Ms. Marcus and she
    nodded.

Go on, Lonnie.

So I read the poem about birth, real slow, the way
Ms. Marcus said
we should read our poetry,
so everybody could understand it.
After I finished, nobody said anything for a long time.
Then the newsman started grinning
Ms. Marcus smiled and the newsman
just sort of shook his head, nodding and looking at me.
Then Lamont said
That poem's corny. It don't even rhyme.
But Angel said *I liked it.* And some other kids said
Me too.

Easter Sunday

At church, the preacher goes on about Christ rising
back up. There's palms everywhere and Easter
lilies in big pots. Everybody's dressed all nice—
ladies in big hats,
guys in suits. Little girls in pink and yellow and white
dresses like Easter eggs.

Was it a big sacrifice to give your life
if you knew you was gonna rise back up?
I mean, isn't that like just taking a nap?

I listen to the preacher. I listen to the people going
Amen and *Yes, Lord.* I run my hand across
Lili's Bible. Some days I feel like I don't know
nothing about nothing.

RODNEY

He comes in the door and sets a big duffel bag down,
lifts Miss Edna up like she weighs two pounds
and she's laughing
and punching
his shoulders and crying all at the same time.
Then he lifts me up, says *Look at Little Brother Lonnie*
all growed up
You almost a man now, aren't you.

Little brother.
Little brother Lonnie.
My big brother Rodney.
Imagine that!

There's roast beef and ribs and potato salad.
There's rice and peas and corn bread and greens.
There's sweet potatoes and macaroni and cheese and
even some fried okra
There's three kinds of pie and two kinds of cake
and we eat
and we eat and we eat till the thought of eating
another bite makes us feel like crying.
All the while Rodney's telling us how he's come on home,
gonna get himself a job here. Says
Ain't nothing for me upstate anymore.
He has Miss Edna's dark skin and straight teeth. They

even laugh the same.
He's tall and his shoulders are wide like somebody
who could
get a pro football contract if they wanted to.
I lift my own skinny shoulders, wishing they'd spread
out like Rodney's do.

Little Brother, he called me.

The kitchen is warm.
Miss Edna can't stop grinning.
Rodney's voice sounds like it should always be
in this house.

Little Brother, he called me.
Little Brother Lonnie.

EPITAPH POEM

for Mama

Liliana C. Motion
Born in October
died in December
But that's not all
that I remember.

FIREFLY

It's almost May
and yesterday
I saw a firefly.

You don't see
them a lot
in the city.

Sometimes
in the park
in the near dark

one comes out
you'll hear
a little kid shout

Lightning bug! Firefly!

It's almost May
and yesterday
I caught a firefly in my hand.

First firefly I
seen in a
long, long time.

Make a wish,
Miss Edna said.
Make a good one.

Firefly wishes always come true.

THE FIRE

The newspapers said it was electrical
bad wiring in the basement or maybe the first floor.
We lived on the third.
Five rooms counting the kitchen
and the kitchen was big.
The newspapers said two people died
and right on the next line was their names.
The newspapers said survived by
Lili and Lonnie Motion. Ages 4 and 7.
A bus was leaving real early for the Bronx Zoo
and Mama and Daddy had a date by themselves
Pastor Marshall's daughter was taking a bunch of kids
so we all slept over at her house
And Mama and Daddy had a date
That made me and Lili laugh
Married people don't go on dates, I said.
And Mama and Daddy shooed us on out of the house
into Pastor Marshall's daughter Sarah's car.
You two be good, Mama said.
And Lili blew her a kiss.

You think it's still flying through the air somewhere?

Almost
Summer Sky

It was the trees first, Rodney tells me.
It's raining out. But the rain is light and warm.
And the sky's not all close to us like it gets
sometimes. It's way up there with
some blue showing through.
Late spring sky, Ms. Marcus says. *Almost summer sky.*
And when she said that, I said
Hey Ms. Marcus, that's a good title
for a poem, right?
You have a poet's heart, Lonnie.
That's what Ms. Marcus said to me.
I have a poet's heart.
That's good. A good thing to have.
And I'm the one who has it.

Now Rodney puts his arm around my shoulder
We keep walking. There's a park
eight blocks from Miss Edna's house
That's where we're going.
Me and Rodney to the park.
Rain coming down warm
Rodney with his arm around my shoulder
Makes me think of Todd and his pigeons
how big his smile gets when they fly.

The trees upstate ain't like other trees you seen, Lonnie
Rodney squints up at the sky, shakes his head
smiles.
No, upstate they got maple and catalpa and scotch pine,
all kinds of trees just standing.
Hundred-year-old trees big as three men.

When you go home this weekend, Ms. Marcus said.
Write about a perfect moment.

Yeah, Little Brother, Rodney says.
You don't know about shade till you lived upstate.
Everybody should do it—even if it's just for a little while.

Way off, I can see the park—blue-gray sky
touching the tops of trees.

I had to live there awhile, Rodney said.
Just to be with all that green, you know?
I nod, even though I don't.
I can't even imagine moving away from here,
from Rodney's arm around my shoulder,
from Miss Edna's Sunday cooking,
from Lily in her pretty dresses and great
big smile when she sees me.

Can't imagine moving away

From
Home.

You know what I love about trees, Rodney says.
It's like . . . It's like their leaves are hands reaching
out to you. Saying Come on over here, Brother.
Let me just . . . Let me just . . .
Rodney looks down at me and grins.
Let me just give you some shade for a while.

CLYDE POEM 1:
DOWN SOUTH

They used to live in Macon, Georgia
Peaches, he says. *Georgia pecans you eat right
off the tree. Georgia pines like those that don't grow
no place else.*

He picks up little rocks and throws them across the
  school yard.

I know Georgia, I say. *I know all about those pecans and
  pine trees.*

The sun is warm and bright yellow.
There's kids screaming everywhere.

But me and Clyde don't hardly notice
'Cause we're sitting up against the school yard fence
just slow-pitching little stones

and remembering Georgia

a place we both used to
a long time ago know.

First Day
of School

When Eric comes back, it's like the first day
of school and he's the new boy
in a classroom where everybody's been together since
kindergarten. He's skinnier, quieter
and everybody looks at him out of the corner
of their eyes. Even Lamont is looking
away when he slaps Eric's hand and says
What's up, Dog?
And even Eric's not looking at anything when he says
Ain't nothing so softly, you wonder
what happened to the other Eric.

And at lunchtime Eric shakes his head no
when we ask him to play ball,
walks real slow over to the edge of the school yard
and sits by himself
just staring like he's been
dropped out of the sky
into a world that's kind of familiar
but mostly not.

What's up, Dog? We say to him
and he just looks off, nods real slow
like he's seen some things

we've never seen.
Knows some things
we'll never know.

DEAR GOD

Dear God,

I'm reading the book you wrote. My sister, Lili, gave it to me. I like the beginning when it talks about how you made everything and then rested. It don't say how though. Like how *did* you make the sky and the water and the earth and stuff? And when you took a rib from Adam to make Eve, was that like an operation? Miss Edna says it's blasphemous to ask those kinds of questions but I just wouldn't mind knowing some answers. Lili said when I finish the book, we'll be back together. It won't be exactly the same 'cause, as you know, my mom and dad passed away. You must know because people blame you. I mean, people always say "The Lord works in mysterious ways" and that makes me think that them dying in that fire had something to do with you. I don't really understand though. So I'm trying to finish up the book you wrote but it's got a lot of pages and a lot of names I can't sound out. I read a little bit every night and when Miss Edna comes in, she nods at me and smiles. In the nighttime if she hears me crying, she comes in and rubs my shoulders. She says, "It's gonna be okay, Lonnie. Don't you worry none. It's all gonna work out fine." And some nights, I fall asleep believing her. God? Did you know that this was a poem letter? And God? Is there some kinda sign you can send down about how Mama and Daddy are doing up there with you? I'm gonna see Lili tomorrow and it'd be nice to go to her new mama's house with some good news.

Love, Lonnie.

LaTenya II

"All, all, all in together girls
how you like the weather, girls?
Fine. Fine. Superfine.
January, February, March . . ."

That's how the jump-rope song goes.
LaTenya's over there. She jumps out
on her birthday month, March,
comes over to where I'm sitting
against the school yard fence.

LaTenya! one of the other girls says but LaTenya
just waves her hand
I'm done playing, she says. Then sits down
says *Hey.*

I say *Hey yourself.*
My stupid heart beating hard.
LaTenya so close I can smell coconut hair grease
like the kind Miss Edna uses sometimes.

I can see a place on her hand where a little bump
     sticks out
right by her pinky finger.
What's that? I ask, pointing.
And LaTenya puts her hands real fast behind her back.

Then after a long time, she takes them out again.
Holds them out to show me.
Used to have extra fingers, she says.
You gonna run away now?
You gonna call me a freak?

The school yard's sunny and loud.
There's kids everywhere.

LaTenya's friends start singing that *All, all*
all in together, girls song again.
I want to say You sure are beautiful, LaTenya.
I want to say You sure are something.
But my lips get stuck over my teeth.
And my mouth dries up.

And all I can do is reach out and touch
those tiny bumps that once was fingers
look at LaTenya, smile and let out a little whisper

No.

JUNE

Camp Kaufman's in upstate New York
in a little town with a long name.
You go to Port Authority and take a bus
and ride for two hours.
Then you're there.
And there's horses and a lake, a swimming pool too.
And there's your little sister, Lili
for two whole weeks in July
the two of you with a whole lot of other kids
but the *two of you*
together again
every single day.
Camp Kaufman's coming

But now it's June
and you're walking in Prospect Park
with your little sister, Lili,
her new mama's back there at a picnic table
with some people from her church
that you go to now
every other Sunday not because of church
or her new mama's god
or the Bible your sister gave you.
You go because her new mama said *Well, I guess so*
when you asked if you could start going.

You go because
you get to sit next to your little sister
for two whole hours and after, if the weather's nice
you and your little sister get to go to Prospect Park
and spend some more time

together.

Some of the church ladies pinch your cheek
Say *He's a handsome boy, Selma*
to Lili's new mama
who just gives you that look
And sweet as he can be, the church ladies say.

It's Sunday
and you and your little sister are walking in the park.
It's warm and the sun is too bright to look up at
but you feel it on your forehead and neck and down
    your arms.

Later on, maybe you and your big brother Rodney'll go
shoot some hoops
and Rodney will laugh when you tell him
about the church ladies.
As sweet as he can be, you'll say
tryna sound just like them
And Rodney will throw his head back
laugh his big laugh.

But right now, your little sister's saying
I told you and holding tight to your hand.
Right now, your little sister's just skipping along
beside you. *I told you, Lonnie!*

You see God everywhere these days. Especially
when Miss Edna makes her sweet potato pie
and when
your little sister smiles.

And camp is only another three weeks away.
And school is almost over.

Maybe one day I'll see your name in print
Ms. Marcus said.
You have a gift, Lonnie.

The poems come to you day and night. Sometimes
they wake you up
and make you write them down real fast even though
there's not a voice saying *Be quiet, Lonnie* in your head
anymore
Just words.
Lots and lots and lots of words and

this sunny day already making itself into a poem
about your beautiful sister, Lili
skipping beside you in her yellow dress
Smiling 'cause you finally finished reading the Bible
she gave you

the Bible she thinks is the reason you two
are here now

together

You let her go on thinking that
'cause she's just a little kid
and you're her big brother, Locomotion
who'd do anything
to keep her smiling.

I told you. I told you, she keeps saying.

This day is already putting all kinds of words
in your head
and breaking them up into lines
and making the lines into pictures in your mind
And in the pictures the people are
laughing and frowning and
eating and reading and
playing ball and skipping along and

spinning themselves into poetry.

And I was right, Lili says, looking up at me. *Wasn't I?*

ACKNOWLEDGMENTS

Thanks so much to Juliet Widoff, Nancy Paulsen, Kimiko Hahn, Reiko Hahn-Hannan, and Toshi Reagon for—among other things—reading this.

And a huge shout-out of thanks to all of my friends who are poets, especially Meg Kearney, who helped me enormously with line breaks and forms and whose kind words made me believe, all over again, in the power of poetry.

Literature Circles

Use these questions and the activities that follow to get more out of the experience of reading *Locomotion* by Jacqueline Woodson.

1. What is Lonnie's full name, and how did he get his name?

2. Lonnie writes about sometimes going to the drugstore to smell the honeysuckle talcum powder. Why does he do this?

3. Though Lonnie doesn't live with his sister anymore, he often writes about her. What kind of brother is Lonnie to his sister Lili? How do we know?

4. Why do you think Lonnie is so irritated with Ms. Marcus—his favorite teacher—when she assigns the class to write about their families?

5. Miss Edna is overjoyed because her son Rodney is coming back to the city to live. How does Lonnie feel about Rodney, and what role does Rodney end up playing in Lonnie's life?

6. How does Lonnie react when he hears that Eric, his classmate who has often been mean to him, is hospitalized with sickle cell anemia? What can we tell about Lonnie from the way he responds to this news?

7. When his friends are trying to outdo one another with tall tales of the strange things they've seen, Lonnie just says, "Never seen nothing." Why doesn't he talk about his family tragedy with his friends? Do you think he should be more open? Can you imagine how you would be, in Lonnie's shoes?

8. Lili gives Lonnie her Bible and often talks about God with him. Why do you think it is so important to Lili for her brother to "find God"? Do you think Lonnie "finds God" as his sister hopes?

9. Lonnie writes four poems about Clyde, the new boy in his class. Why do you think he is so fascinated by Clyde? Do you think he relates to Clyde in any way?

10. When Lonnie is in church with Miss Edna, he writes the word *HOPE* on his hand. What do you think this means? Why does he do this, and what does this have to do with the other experiences he has?

11. Throughout the book, Lonnie's idea of home starts to change. What does home mean to Lonnie at the end of the book? How do his ideas about this seem to change as he stays longer with Miss Edna?

12. Besides learning about all kinds of poems, from haiku to epistle poems, what does Lonnie learn about writing from Ms. Marcus?

13. Imagine Lonnie's life five or ten years after the end of *Locomotion* and make some predictions about his future. Who or what does Lonnie care about? Who are his friends? Does he still write? What kind of person is he?

14. Do you think Miss Edna is a good foster mother to Lonnie? Did your ideas about her change as you read the book? Give examples from the story to support your answer.

15. As you read, did you admire Lonnie in any way? What do you like best about Lonnie? Would you want him as your friend?

Note: These questions are keyed to Bloom's taxonomy as follows: Knowledge: 1–2; Comprehension: 3–5; Application: 6–7; Analysis: 8–11; Synthesis: 12–13; Evaluation: 14–15

Activities

1. Throughout the book, Lonnie is encouraged by his fifth grade teacher, Ms. Marcus, who really makes an impact on him. Imagine that Ms. Marcus is writing an email or letter to another teacher friend in which she describes her fifth grade class, including Lonnie. What would she say about Lonnie and about his class? How does she view her job as a teacher? Write a letter as if you are Ms. Marcus, and share your thoughts and feelings about your job, your class, and Lonnie.

2. Lonnie's story in *Locomotion* is not told in chronological order; instead Lonnie tells his story as the memories come to him. Create a timeline of his life, starting with his birth and going up to fifth grade, using as many of the events from the novel as you can in the order they happened. Illustrate your timeline with small pictures or symbols for each event, and use a color key to show what each experience meant to Lonnie. For example, you might write his painful experiences in red, his happy experiences in yellow, and his learning experiences in green.

3. Try to imitate Lonnie's poetic style. Choose a memory or story of your own, and write it like he does in a few, carefully-chosen words. Try to pay attention to spacing and line breaks, and give your poem a title. When you're finished, illustrate your poem, using colors to show the mood your poem portrays.

Other Books by this Author

Novels: *If You Come Softly, Hush, Last Summer with Maizon, I Hadn't Meant to Tell You This, Miracle's Boys* (all published by Putnam).

Author Website: www.jacquelinewoodson.com